THE ALIEN PROMISE

GRACE KENSINGTON

1

———

I didn't know how to feel or what to do. I stood at the doorway to the house, what was meant to be my new home, staring into the darkness for what felt like hours after Bannack left. Finally I stepped back into the house and closed the door behind me, pressing my back against it and sliding to the floor so that I could curl my knees against my chest and rest my forehead against my folded arms. Everything around me in the Denynso compound was strange and unknown, and now suddenly I was feeling a pain that I never knew existed, with an intensity that was far beyond anything I thought that I could ever feel. The air around me felt oppressive, while the places on my body that Bannack had touched now felt cold and abandoned. I felt empty inside, both in that my heart felt torn from my chest and in that my body still ached for him even though he had left so abruptly. I couldn't understand what had just happened.

I sat against the door, letting the darkness of the coming night close in around me without moving to turn on any of the lights throughout the space. Everything had been going so perfectly. The feelings that I had experienced for Bannack since the first moment that I saw him had grown within me until they felt like they were burning in my belly and overflowing within my chest, creating a sense that made me at once overwhelmed and elated. I had been so young when the rest of my kind had died off due to the horrific plague that scourged our home that I had never had the opportunity to feel love, or even real attraction, to anyone. I had seen my parents together and how they felt about each other was obvious. I could remember even then how they would hold hands, gaze at each other, and find any excuse to be close to each other, even after they had spent more than half of their lives together. I hadn't understood that until I had seen Bannack.

Being alone in the mirrored realm that existed beneath the Denynso compound had been isolating and lonely, but I had grown accustomed to my life alone underground. Over the years I had become absolutely comfortable with not having anyone else with me, and even felt that I preferred the quiet and isolation because it meant that I could live exactly as I wanted to and have no one and nothing to tell me otherwise. When the Klimnu invaded, the terror had been more that they would change my lifestyle than that they would hurt me, and I had managed to stay completely out of the way the entire time that they were down there. Even when I saw the human woman and the Denynso traitor, and then the other human women, come into the mirrored realm, I felt no compulsion to interact with them. I had hoped that the Klimnu would simply tire of my world and leave me alone so that I could go back to my simple, independent life and not have to worry about anything else.

The moment that my eyes touched Bannack, however, all of that changed. Everything around him disappeared. I couldn't perceive the other warriors or the slimy, disgusting creatures that were battling them. It was as though nothing else in the entire world mattered in those moments but this beautiful warrior who in a single second changed everything about how I felt about life. Suddenly I didn't want to live completely alone underground anymore. I didn't want to continue on with the lifestyle that I had built and evolved into after my family and friends had died. I didn't want to be left to my own devices, or to have a life that was totally my own. In that instant I could understand why my parents spent nearly all of their time together, and why when my father died, my mother followed him only hours later even though she had barely been sick.

He, of course, didn't know it, but I had watched the entire battle between the Klimnu and the Denynso. I had followed him carefully in each of his movements, making sure that he stayed safe as he fought. I didn't even know his name then, but I could feel the intensity of his presence and the energy emanating off of him in a way that I had never experienced. In the final moments of the battle, I had saved him. He stumbled while trying to approach Jem, the incredibly courageous warrior who had given his life to ensure the future of his people, and a moment later caught himself. He thought that he had simply managed to find his footing and regain his hold on the vine that was coming from the tree where he stood. In reality, I had reflected the surface of the tree so that he could step steadily onto it before finding his way back to his original stance.

The action had been risky. I nearly betrayed my existence in that single moment, but I was willing to do anything in order to ensure that he got through the battle safely. It was a decision that I had made impulsively, without really thinking, and it hadn't struck me until I saw him again the next day and had the compulsion to again save him from tumbling into the reflection of the sky by creating a floor of the image of the stone wall that it was him that I had saved. It was as if I was reacting to a memory that I hadn't made yet, a thought or a feeling that I had deep within me that wasn't really there but was waiting to be there. It was difficult even for me to explain, but something that I wanted to feel more of.

The glow of my skin was even more evident in the room now that I was cloaked in complete darkness and I thought about the first time that Bannack saw me. He had felt something when he got down into the mirrored realm. Something within him had told him that things were changing and that he was about to experience something that would forever change him, but no matter how hard I tried to look into him, I couldn't figure out exactly what that was. When he noticed my glow across the sky, however, that feeling had intensified and I knew that he felt the same draw and need about me that I was feeling about him.

He had trusted me then. He had given himself over to me and to the unknown that waited when he took a completely unafraid step away from the branches that crossed the reflected sky and created the only source of stability that they knew down in my world, and onto the stone floor that I had made for him. There had been no sense of fear in him, or even unsureness. It was as though he knew, even if he had no concept of what or who I was, that he was safe as long as I was there.

What had happened between that moment and the moment when he ran out of the house and into the darkness of the night without a single word of explanation? He had taken my hand in my world beneath the compound, led me out of the ground and literally into a world that I had never once seen or experienced. I had offered myself to him in the way that he had offered himself to me, stepping into something that I had only heard about and never once witnessed myself, for the first time in my solitary existence truly wanting to go above ground, and for the first time in the years since I had become accustomed to being alone that I had wanted to put that life behind me and share life with someone else.

In those moments I felt a connection between us that was only growing with each second. Resistance had begun to build inside him, though, and he had started to fight the feelings that I knew he had when he looked at me. He didn't need to say them. I could feel them when he touched me, when he rested his mouth to mine, and when he tucked his hand between my thighs to create unimaginable sensations and emotions within me. Just before I welcomed his body into mine, however, he moved me off of him and started to dress. I had dropped my dress over my head and tied the laces as quickly as I could, but it wasn't fast enough to stop him from crossing to the door, his shirt clutched in his hand, and running out into the darkness of the compound.

My own voice screaming after him was reverberating in my mind and tears like I hadn't cried since I was a small child pooled beneath my eyes and poured down the skin of my arms where my head rested. He had given me no explanation, offered no reason for suddenly leaving me in the silence aching for him, but in that moment I felt more alone than I ever had.

2

—————

Bannack paced outside of the bakery for a few minutes, not really knowing what he was supposed to do with himself, and trying to convince himself that the decision he had made was the right one. After all, he had been the one to bring up the fact that the Denynso, including Creia, the king who they all looked up to and thought of as being the most powerful and knowledgeable of them all, didn't really know anything about the rest of the planet of Uoria or what types of species inhabited their planet. It had been this assertion and his insistence that they find out what was going on that brought them back down into the mirrored realm that they had discovered during the final battle with the Klimnu. If that hadn't happened, they never would have found Loralia at all, and the rest of the warriors, particularly Pyra, wouldn't have agreed with him about how important it was to go out and find out more about the planet.

The fact that the warriors were now planning on leaving the compound for the first time and going on an exploration of the rest of the planet so that they could see what they might discover and potentially identify future threats to them was based entirely on his determination and his recommendations. It was only logical and fair that he be permitted to go along with them. He had not asked Loralia to request him as her guard and protector while she was in the compound. While he had been the one who had asked her to come up above ground in the compound with them, it had not been his idea for the king and queen to invite her to stay with them once they found out that she was the only one left of her kind. He should not be held responsible for the wellbeing of a creature who he didn't know and who he had not pledged his loyalty to until forced.

The more he paced and the harder he thought, the closer Bannack was to convincing himself that asking the human women to take on the responsibilities of taking care of Loralia and making sure that she got assimilated to her new surroundings so that he could join the other warriors in the quest outside the compound was not only fair, but truly his only choice. If he had agreed to stay behind with Loralia rather than going with Pyra, Gyyx, Ero, and the others, he would have compromised his position as a warrior and presented himself as being a coward. He also would have shorted himself an opportunity to learn things that no other Denynso had ever known, possibly putting himself and the rest of the compound at risk should he ever come into contact with one of the species that the warriors found during their explorations.

Even though he had made himself believe he was fully justified in walking away from his responsibilities with Loralia, he still couldn't entirely convince himself that walking away from her, or more precisely running away from her, after he brought her home was the right thing to do. He was incredibly torn, more conflicted than he had ever been in his entire life. Loralia was the single most beautiful thing that he had ever seen, and even before he had laid eyes on her, his mind and body had started responding to her presence. Just being near her made his defensive, aggressive instincts kick in stronger than they ever had even in the many battles he had faced. As soon as he saw her, he was instantly entranced by her. She was ethereal and gorgeous in a way that was truly indescribable. The gentle glow of her skin, incomparable lavender color of her eyes, and flowing silver hair made her look as though she were not quite real, as if she were a delightful figment of his imagination conjured in a moment of near-death to soothe and comfort him.

The touch of her hand and the smell of her skin, though, told him that she was absolutely not a figment of his imagination or some wonderfully lucid dream. She was incredibly real, real in a way that he could not quite fathom and was not ready to believe. Loralia created in Bannack feelings that he didn't want to admit to himself much less anyone else, and the more he felt them, the more he wanted to force them down into himself so that they couldn't be felt, seen, or experienced. This was not the way it was supposed to be. He had not waited his entire life to find his mate only to find himself falling for a creature that belonged to a species he hadn't even known existed until that day.

He hated himself for the betrayal of his mind and body, and for not being able to control himself. He hated himself even more than that lack of control had led him to nearly mating with her. If he had waited just seconds longer he would have felt her body envelope him, and he would have known for sure if she was what he feared his mind was trying to tell him that she was. Bannack had not been ready for that moment of clarity. He didn't know which answer he dreaded more, or how he would have responded to either one. In that moment all he knew was that he needed to get away from her, and that he didn't want to be in the same room with her again for a very long time.

Even as he thought that, though, he knew that he was lying to himself. No matter how hard the two sides of him struggled and fought, he couldn't deny that he still felt incredibly drawn to Loralia, and that more than anything he wanted to be near her.

"Bannack."

He heard Eden's voice from behind him and he turned to look at her. She had her hand rested protectively over her swollen belly like she usually did and the little bit of weight that she had gained in her face during her pregnancy made her look softer and gentler than she had when she first arrived on the planet.

"What's going on with you?" Eden asked, lowering her voice as though she wanted to keep the conversation private.

"What do you mean?" Bannack asked, trying to force his voice to sound casual.

"I know you, Bannack. I know when you aren't telling the whole truth, and right now a big part of you is lying. Asking me and the other girls to take care of Loralia isn't just about wanting to go wander around the planet with the other warriors. What is it actually about?"

Sometimes Bannack really hated how in tune to emotions that the human women seemed to be. The Denynso women weren't like that. They were gentler and more feeling than the men tended to be, but they were still aggressive and gruff compared to the humans. He could only imagine how much more difficult it was for their Denynso mates. Part of the mating process for their kind was creating an unbreakable link during the actual bonding.

This link made it possible for the mates to communicate with one another without having to speak, which meant that not only were the human women able to tell when their mates were dealing with an emotional situation, they could actually read their thoughts and find out exactly what was going on if the Denynso men weren't careful to control what was going through their minds. It seemed overwhelming to be that close to someone else.

"I just want to go with the other warriors," he said, "It was my idea to find out more about the other species anyway."

He realized that he sounded like he was whining, but he didn't really care. He was dealing with enough of his own confused thoughts and feelings to think about trying to seem tough and put together.

"Alright. Don't tell me if you don't want to. Just know that I know that there is something else going on, and eventually we are going to all figure it out."

She turned and headed back into the bakery. Bannack had absolutely no doubt that what the little red-haired human woman had said was the truth. They were smart, crafty, and extremely capable. Not only could they find out what he was going through if they wanted to, they would, and they would do their best to interfere until they helped him find a solution. That just meant he needed to get out of the compound and away from Loralia as quickly as possible.

3

I don't know how long I sat on the floor, my back against the door to the house that was meant to be my home but was feeling more and more like a strange and unwelcoming prison with every second. Part of me wanted so much to go out into the compound and look for Bannack so that I could ask him what happened and hope that he could give me some explanation for running away from me like that. Maybe there was an element of his species that I didn't know about that had made him leave. He had asked me if I had read his mind, and he seemed frustrated and almost angry when he asked me. Perhaps there was something more to that question than I had originally thought. If the people of this species could easily communicate with each other through their minds, it was possible that one of them had reached out to Bannack and told him that he was needed somewhere else. The loyalty and sense of duty that came with being a warrior would mean that he felt compelled and inarguably obligated to go where he was needed.

Though it didn't fully explain why Bannack hadn't

responded to me when I called for him after he left, or why he didn't simply tell me why he was leaving, telling myself that there could be an explanation behind his sudden departure did soothe me in a way. I still felt hurt and upset, not so much angry as I was simply brokenhearted. I knew that the feelings that had built inside me so intensely happened very quickly, but I had never once felt like they were forced or that I was moving beyond what he was feeling as well. In that moment it struck me that even though I hadn't thought that I was moving too quickly, my understanding of the love and relationship rituals of my own kind was minimal, and I knew absolutely nothing about the relationships of the Denynso. I realized that it was possible that I had offended him in some way, and that thought made me feel sick to my stomach. The idea that in my haste to explore what I was feeling toward him I had pushed my warrior away and ended the possibility that we would ever be together made me wish that I had never come above ground.

I was just beginning to stand up, planning to go to sleep and see how I felt about everything in the light of the morning, when I heard a knock on the door behind me. My heart jumped in my chest. I hoped that it was Bannack, come back to explain what happened and perhaps resume where we had left off. I straightened my dress, smoothed away the last of the tears that were still lingering on my cheeks, and opened the door. As soon as I did, the smile faded from my face. Instead of Bannack standing outside, it was two of the human women that I had met when they came underground with the warriors along with one who had been in the meeting hall when Bannack brought me to meet the king and queen of their people.

The expression on my face must have given away my

disappointment at seeing them rather than Bannack because they all narrowed their eyes slightly and looked concerned.

"Is everything alright?" the one I remembered as Zuri asked.

I nodded, trying to muster a smile that would assure them that I was fine.

"Are you sure?" the lovely, rather heavily pregnant one asked.

If it was possible, her belly looked slightly more swollen than when I had first seen her and I could feel that she was tired and somewhat anxious. I could only imagine that carrying a child at all would be stressful, but I had also noticed that there didn't seem to be any other pregnant women, babies, or children at all throughout the compound. The youngest people I had seen were some of the warriors who looked only a few years younger than me.

"Is there something wrong with the house? Are the lights not turning on?" Zuri asked.

All of the attention coming from them was becoming overwhelming and I felt bombarded even though I knew that they had come to me out of concern and genuine desire to welcome me to the compound. I stepped back and held out a hand to invite them to come inside.

"Everything is fine," I told them, "I haven't turned on any of the lights yet."

The faint light emanating from my skin and the blue glow coming from a luminescent plant across the room filled the space with just enough illumination that I was able to see the women clearly as they came into the room. I crossed to one of the lamps sitting on a low table that was similar to the types of lights that I had down in the mirrored realm and touched its base, hoping that it would turn on, which it did. The new light in the room seemed to put the women slightly more at ease and they all came further into the room.

They didn't want to say it, and they tried very much to be as subtle as they could, but they were all scrutinizing me closely as they approached. Though they were happy to welcome me into the compound and do whatever they could to help me assimilate, they were also somewhat wary of me, an emotion that each carried in a slightly different way.

I could feel that Zuri focused heavily on the way that I looked, identifying the differences between us and feeling at once uncomfortable and guilty about that feeling. The image of Ero, a man I assumed to be her mate, flickered through her mind and the discomfort eased. Leia, the smallest of the women, was fascinated by my differences, but also carried a sense of defensiveness and distance that came from dark memories of the first time she encountered a species that was not her own, dark memories that she shielded closely within her.

The pregnant woman was the most difficult. She was at the same moment the one who seemed most willing to welcome me and the most nurturing, but also the most hesitant. Carrying the child within her had heightened both her natural sense of curiosity and desire to learn about the world around her, but also of fear and suspicion. I could sense that as much as she wanted to think of me as just another woman who had found her way into the Denynso compound, she was also nervous about encountering another species that she didn't understand and that she had had no time to learn to trust.

This was perhaps the most difficult part of being around other creatures again. When I was alone I had no one's emotions to contend with but my own. I could feel and experience only what was impacting me at that moment and work through them in the way that was right for me. When I was with others, I could feel and experience what they did, forcing me to acknowledge their true impressions of me and of the world around them. While it was possible for me to control it and block myself from reflecting the thoughts and feelings of others, I had never built that skill when I was younger and now it was an incredible challenge for me to not tune in to others when I was struggling with my own emotions. This meant that right when I was at my most vulnerable, my mind betrayed me and allowed even more emotion in, often putting me in painful, difficult moments when I was at my least capable of tolerating them.

"I'm Eden," the pregnant woman said, stepping toward me cautiously, "I don't think that I've introduced myself yet."

"Hello," I said, "I'm Loralia."

"I know. We just wanted to come see you and let you know that we're excited that you decided to stay with us. There aren't enough ladies around here."

The three women laughed and I felt myself smile. Despite their hesitance, it was nice to hear that they were happy that I was there.

"Thank you."

"We know what it's like to leave the home you've always known and suddenly become a part of the Denynso," Eden continued, "and we want you to know that we're here for you and we're looking forward to spending time with you while Bannack is gone."

She gave me a soft hint of a knowing smile, but I couldn't even force one back at her.

"What do you mean while Bannack is gone?" I asked,

barely able to push the words through the hard lump forming in my throat.

Eden, Zuri, and Leia looked struck and exchanged glances.

"He didn't tell you?" Leia asked.

"No."

"He is leaving with the warriors."

                                    4

                          ____

Bannack walked into the meeting hall with a sense
of relief, but at the same time, a feeling of longing
and emptiness that made him wish that he could
simply turn off his emotions and face the world completely
blank and cold. It was that way that the warriors marched
into their battles, emotionless, aggressive, and without
feeling or compassion. He wished that he could maintain
that throughout the rest of his life as well so that he didn't
have to deal with feeling like this anymore.

It made him feel better to know that Eden, Zuri, and
Leia had gone to see Loralia and welcome her to the
compound, but he knew that them going to see her meant
that she would soon know that he was leaving and aban-
doning his guard and protector responsibilities. He knew
that this was going to hurt her, and as much as he was
conflicted about how he was feeling about her, he hated the
idea that he was causing this creature that had already gone
through so much even more pain. He didn't want to be her
impression of life above the ground, but he didn't have a
choice. He had made a single impulsive decision by walking

out across the sky and toward the pearlescent glow that had seemed to call to him, and in that decision he felt like he had given over control of himself.

He no longer felt like he could think clearly or make the types of rational decisions that he once did. Though volatile and unpredictable, Bannack had always been one to understand his own motivations and compulsions, even if none of the other warriors, men, women, or even rulers of the Denynso understood them. He didn't like the feeling that these were things he couldn't think his way through and that for the first time his heart seemed to be making decisions that his mind didn't understand or condone.

Some of the other warriors were milling around in the meeting hall talking about the upcoming trip. A few of them were still questioning the decision to leave the compound and go on the quest, and others were trying to convince them that it was the right thing for the entirety of the clan. Bannack had no interest in trying to build up their ranks or muster more support for the trip, especially if that meant delaying their departure more than the three days that they already had planned. He simply wanted to get their plans in place, prepare, and leave.

Bannack felt a hard pat on his back and spun around defensively, taking an aggressive step forward even before he saw who was standing behind him. Ty, a gentle giant in every meaning of the phrase, stepped back, a startled look in his deep orange eyes. The shade of his eyes was a recent development, a color that had formed only in the couple of weeks since the massive baker had discovered his mate in the beautiful, brilliant, and very young Samira.

"I'm sorry," Bannack said, shaking slightly to try to release the tension that had built in his body.

He felt like he had been wound up, the pressure inside

him building almost unbearably and just waiting for its release. It was similar to the feeling that he got when they were marching toward battle, but deeper and more intense in a way that he couldn't quite understand and hadn't ever experienced.

"Are you doing OK, Bannack?" Ty asked, "You haven't really seemed like yourself since the funeral."

Bannack wanted to brush off the comment and just try to pass it off as being devastated over Jem's death like the rest of the tribe, but he knew that that wouldn't work. Ty, like the others, had known Bannack their entire lives and it would take much more than a flimsy excuse to get them off of his back if they really wanted to know what was going on with him. He let Ty guide him over to one of the long tables where no one else was sitting and slumped down onto the bench.

"I can't think straight," Bannack admitted, "I feel like my mind is going in a thousand different directions and all I want to do is get on our way so that I don't have to think anymore. Why do we have to wait three days?"

"Because it's going to take that long to get all of the supplies together that we need. Besides, we want a little bit of time to say goodbye to our mates properly. It might be a while before we see them again and we'd like to make sure that we have plenty to think about while we're gone."

The young man gave a laugh, but Bannack couldn't muster the same reaction. He glanced down at his hands, suddenly feeling even more uncomfortable at the mention of the other men's mates.

"What are you thinking about so hard over here, Bannack?"

Pyra and Ero came up and settled onto the benches, Ero beside Bannack and Pyra across the table from him beside

Ty. All three of the men were staring at him, and Bannack felt the same desperate need to get away that he had when he was standing at the funeral. He knew that that was not really an option now, however. He looked into the faces of each of the men and thought that perhaps talking to them might be a good thing. It could help him to sort through whatever was running through his mind and gain some clarity so that he knew how to move forward.

"I just can't seem to get a hold of my brain recently."

"Why not? Is something going on?" Ero asked.

"I just have all these thoughts and I've been feeling particularly aggressive and angry lately. Ever since the battle, I just feel like I can't keep control of myself."

Out of the corner of his eye Bannack saw the other men exchange glances.

"Are you feeling like you want to kick the living hell out of just about every guy that gets near you, including us?"

"Well, I did just almost punch Ty in the face because he came up and patted me on the back."

"And are you having any other interesting changes? Physical changes, perhaps?"

Bannack squirmed on the bench. He was rethinking how good of an idea it actually was to get the other men involved in this conversation. Ero glanced down at Bannack's lap and Bannack saw him grin and look back at Ty and Pyra.

"I can definitely confirm that he is."

Pyra gave a short, knowing laugh and shook his head at Bannack.

"So who is she?"

Bannack felt his stomach turn. It was exactly what he had been dreading hearing from any of the men. He shook his head, refusing to make eye contact with any of them.

"Come on, tell us," Ty said.

Ty had always been the kindest and most romantic-minded of the Denynso men, a nurturer rather than a warrior though he had recently embraced his incredible inherited power and joined in the final fight against the Klimnu, and looked far more excited about the situation than Bannack felt.

"It has to be one of the Denynso women," Ero speculated, "There haven't been any other girls who have come around here recently."

There was a pause and then Bannack saw Pyra staring at him.

"Except Loralia."

Bannack shook his head again, but there was no use, they had figured it out and now he had nowhere to hide.

"Oh, shit," Ero said, "It is her. You have a thing for the weird little mirror creature."

Bannack knew that he meant it teasingly, but his anger at that statement nearly overwhelmed him. He stood sharply, slamming his hands down in the middle of the table and glaring down at Ero.

"I do not have a 'thing' for her," he snarled.

"Your reactions to her seem to beg to differ," Ty pointed out.

"Have you slept with her? Your eyes aren't orange."

"No, and they wouldn't be even if I had. There's no way that my intended mate is some freakish creature from underground. I am meant to bond with a Denynso woman, like I'm supposed to. I'm not going to fall for some other species, especially one that I know absolutely nothing about."

As soon as the words came out of his mouth, Bannack saw the other men tense. A stiff moment of silence fell over the table as each of them stood slowly from their benches. He met their gazes in turn, seeing a darkness in each of them that he hadn't anticipated.

"Another species?" Pyra snarled, his hand clenching into a fist beside him, "You mean like humans?"

5

I could hear the women still talking around me, but it was as if their voices were lost in some kind of fog that was closing in on me. I was trying desperately to process what they had just told me, but no matter how hard I tried to work through it in my mind, I couldn't force myself to let it sink all the way in.

"Bannack is leaving?"

I repeated my question, hoping that somehow I had mistaken what they had said, but deep down knowing that I had heard them exactly right.

Leia came up beside me and rested a hand on my arm. So small and fragile looking, she had a presence that was strong because it had to be, like a delicate flower that had been forged out of pure steel. It was the fire and chisel that created her as she was.

I felt them guiding me towards the furniture in the middle of the main room of the house, and I allowed them to. I had no reason to distrust these women and in that moment they were my only source of information about Bannack and what was happening around me.

"The warriors have decided to leave the compound and explore the rest of Uoria," Leia explained.

"After the battle with the Klimnu down in the mirrored realm they all realized that none of them, not even the king, knows what the rest of the planet holds, or what types of threats there might be out there. They're unwilling to just sit around and wait to find out if there is another species out there like the Klimnu that might want to destroy the Denynso and take over the compound. It seems that discovering your existence made them even more insistent," Eden said softly.

"Why me?" I asked, looking into each of the women's faces in turn.

"You have lived under the ground that they walked on every single day and they had no idea," Zuri said, "It upsets them that they are known for being the best and most fearsome warriors in all the galaxy, yet they were unable to protect their compound from invasion, and didn't even realize that there was an entire other species living just beneath their feet for as long as they have been around."

"My mate, Pyra," Eden continued, "is especially worried about our child. He or she is the very first child born of this generation of the Denynso, and Pyra doesn't like that he doesn't know what could be out there that might pose a threat to his baby."

"He or she?" I asked.

I had never heard that particular phrase used before, and it struck me as strange that she would use it to refer to her unborn child.

"We don't know what the baby is," Eden explained, "We have no way of knowing. If I were going through my pregnancy back on Earth there would have been ways for me to know long ago if I am having a son or a daughter. The Denynso don't have those ways, though."

There was only a hint of stress in her voice. With the words she had said I would have expected to feel bitterness, or even anger, coming off of her. Instead, I just felt nervousness and the sweeping love that came over her as she mentioned her mate, just like the love that Zuri had felt when she thought of Ero.

"Do you wish that you were back on Earth rather than here with the Denynso?" I asked.

Eden looked at me and shook her head emphatically.

"Absolutely not. Uoria, this compound, is my home, much more so than Earth ever was even though that's where I was born and raised. I didn't know it until I came to this planet as a scientist sent to do a project for work and met Pyra, but this is where I was always meant to be."

I envied the confidence and absolute security that radiated off of her. She had total conviction in what she said, and her heart fully believed every word of it. This really was where she belonged and she couldn't imagine leaving.

"There are other ways than the Earth ways to tell what child you are carrying, you know."

Eden tilted her head quizzically at me and rubbed her belly tenderly.

"The midwives told me that they don't have any kind of technology that can show the baby like they do on Earth, that they take care of it through their own forms of medicine. None of them have ever been able to tell what a woman was having until it was born."

"Ah, but that's the Denynso," I said, smiling for the first time since Bannack had left, "and I'm not a Denynso. My kind has always been able to tell. I could find out for you now if you'd like to know."

Eden nodded and I could feel the hesitance she had felt toward me disappearing. She was learning to trust me, and as she did, the other women did as well. It was a nice feeling, something soothing and comforting in a time when I needed those feelings more than I had in my entire life.

I gestured for Eden to lie down on the couch and I sat beside her, perching just on the edge so that I was close enough to rest my hands on the sides of her swollen belly. It took me a moment to orient myself to the positioning of the baby. Once I did, I reached up to my neck to take my compact, but realized that it wasn't there. I looked around frantically, terrified that I had lost it somewhere between climbing up from out of the ground and removing my dress for Bannack.

Leia dipped down and scooped something up off of the floor.

"Is this what you're looking for?" she asked.

Relief washed over me and I nodded. Before she handed it to me, she opened the sides of the silver compact, revealing the two mirrors within it.

"What is that?" Zuri asked, walking over to look at the compact more closely.

"Please don't touch it," I said sharply when Zuri lifted her fingers to touch the mirrors, "I was born with that compact and I will die with it. If it's broken, there is no way to replace it and I will no longer have the abilities that it gives me."

I hadn't meant to sound angry, but it terrified me to think of my compact getting broken. It was the one remaining link that I had to my family and to my kind. Without it, I would lose everything within me that made me me. I didn't know how to function without it.

"I'm sorry," Leia said, leaning forward to hand me the compact.

"It's alright," I replied, hoping to calm the fear that had started to build in her, "Do you remember when the other woman, Elianna, stepped out onto the floor and it turned back into the sky? I explained that it was a reflection and that she had to believe in what the reflection was showing her in order for it to be real?"

"Yes."

"This," I held up the compact so that she could see it clearly, "is how I made that reflection. This compact enables me to do many things, and one of them will be to tell Eden what type of little one she should be expecting very soon."

The mention of the baby broke the tension in the room and the women all smiled. I opened the compact and placed it with both mirrors flat against Eden's belly close to where I knew the baby's head was positioned. I flattened my palm against the mirror and concentrated on what the mirror was reflecting to me. It was far more difficult to reflect a baby, especially one that was unborn, because they don't know yet how to understand what they are feeling and associate it with concrete thoughts. Instead the compact reflected the essence of the child back to me. This was the inarguable elements of that baby that were stitched into him from the moment of his conception and that would stay with him throughout his entire life. These were the very core of a person, the basic foundation on which all of that person's thoughts, feelings, and perceptions would build.

Having gleaned all I needed to from the reflections of the compact, I closed it, and carefully looped the repaired chain back around my neck. I smiled at Eden.

"You will have a son," I told her, "A boy with the power and spirit of his father, and the strength and courage of his mother. He will have within him the capacity to do amazing things."

Eden had tears sparkling in her eyes and I knew that my description had surprised her. She didn't think of herself as nearly as strong and courageous as she truly was, but I knew that through this baby that she was carrying, one that would be entering the world very soon, that she would learn to see herself in the way that she was made and to see herself in him.

6

Bannack could see the fury in the other men's eyes and he immediately regretted what he had said to them. Not wanting the situation to turn into a conflict within the entire clan, he stepped away from the table and left the meeting hall. Either Pyra, Ero, and Ty would follow him and they would hash through the situation on their own outside, or they wouldn't follow and he could escape into the darkness of the night and deal with his feelings alone like he had been for the last couple of days. He honestly wasn't sure which one of them he would prefer to happen.

As soon as he stepped outside, he realized that the other men had, in fact, followed him and they were seething with so much anger it was almost as though he could feel the waves of energy rolling off of them. He didn't pause on the stairs leading up to the meeting hall but continued down into the center of the compound, bringing him closer to his house and further from the rest of the tribe.

"What did you mean by that?" Ero asked.

The youngest and smallest of the warriors, Ero had

always been teased and bullied for his size. This had made him bitter and angry over the years, creating in him an unpredictable violence that often led him to major conflicts with the other warriors and even non-warrior members of the tribe. When he met Zuri and she became his mate, much of this anger and instability disappeared, replaced by a sense of confidence and control. That new control, however, seemed to be gone now as the temper returned and his eyes flashed aggressively at Bannack.

"I didn't mean anything by it," Bannack said, trying to brush off the comment that he made even though he knew it was completely out of line.

"You obviously meant something by it," Pyra said, stepping closer to Bannack, "You said that there was no way that you were supposed to mate with a species other than the Denynso. Do you think that there is something wrong with other species?"

"It's not that, Pyra," Bannack struggled to find the right words to express what he had been feeling, but they seemed to die and disappear before they could get from his mind to his mouth.

"Well, it seems to be exactly that," Ty said, showing uncharacteristic anger on his face, "It seems like you're saying that the only acceptable mates for us are Denynso women, and that you are too good to have a mate that isn't one of them."

"Let me remind you that each one of us, as well as Gyyx and Ciyrs, found mates that are most certainly not Denynso women. We fell in love with humans, a species that none of us knew anything about any more than you know anything about Loralia's kind."

"You knew something about them," Bannack snapped back, "We have encountered humans before; even had them come and stay with us for a few months at a time. You might not have known a lot about humans before the women came, but you knew something. You had spent time talking with humans and you had heard about them from Creia. They weren't a complete unknown."

"Why does that matter?"

"With Loralia, I know nothing. Absolutely nothing. We didn't even know that there was a species that existed below ground, much less what they are like. So how am I supposed to be OK with the fact that apparently I am falling for her when I don't even know who or what she is? Mating with a Denynso woman would mean that I understood her. I would know what she is, where she came from, and how we were going to live our lives together. We would have a shared history and the same perspectives. It would be easier and more realistic to bond with her and stay bonded with her because we would be able to know each other more quickly and more easily."

"So you think that because our mates are human women and not Denynso women that our bonds are not as close as the men who have Denynso mates? Or that somehow our relationships are not as good, or as 'realistic'?"

"Be honest, Pyra," Bannack said, staring directly into Pyra's raging orange eyes, "Don't you feel better knowing that Eden is technically a Denynso? Didn't it make you happy that Ciyrs somehow changed her from a human to one of us?"

"I was happy that he saved her life and that I wasn't going to have to live without her. I didn't care what she was. All I cared about was that he got the Klimnu toxins out of her and kept her alive. If that meant turning her into a Denynso woman, that was what it would take; but I wouldn't have loved her any less if she had woken up still completely human."

"After everything that's happened in the last few months with the Klimnu and Jem, and now with the idea of going out into the other areas of the planet to find out what else is out there, I just don't think I'm ready to even think about having a mate, much less having one that I will have to learn everything about."

"Do you really think that any of us was really ready when we found our mates? Or that we didn't have to learn everything about them, too?"

"If you haven't noticed, those five women might all be humans, but they are in no way exactly alike. Each one of them is so different it barely even matters that they are the same species," Ty said, "I know that being with Samira doesn't mean that I understand Eden like Pyra does, and that Ero wouldn't be able to trade Zuri for Leia and just expect that Gyyx would be able to pick right up with her without any problem. That's part of finding your mate. You have to learn her and she has to learn you. Remember, you're just as much a different species to Loralia and she is to you."

That statement struck Bannack harder than he would have anticipated it would have. He had been so wrapped up in how conflicted he felt about her that he never stopped to think about how Loralia perceived him. She hadn't shown a single moment of hesitance when it came to him, and had given herself over to her feelings for him immediately, never once worrying that he wasn't one of her kind, or even that he was a part of a species that had taken over the land where her kind used to live, something that the Denynso would have responded to with violence and anger. She had soothed him and offered herself to him in a way that was so trusting it now made him feel sick at the way that he had treated her.

"What am I going to do?" Bannack asked, looking at the men around him.

The anger in their eyes faded and he could see compassion build in their expressions. Each of them had been through their own personal struggle when they were finding their mates, and they knew how difficult it was to overcome those feelings. Ero had even had to go so far as to travel from Uoria to Earth, becoming the first of his kind to ever travel through space, in order to find Zuri and apologize to her after offending and hurting her so deeply that she had left the planet only a day after arriving. They understood what it was like to be unsure of the intense, all-consuming feelings that came with finding their mates, and now he needed them to tell him how to get through it.

"What in the hell is wrong with you?"

A shriek from across the center of the compound pulled Bannack's attention away from the other men and he saw Eden stalking toward him with a ferocious look in her eyes. Somehow her belly made her look even more intimidating, like a mother animal ready to fight something that was threatening her nest. Bannack took a step back, but Pyra stepped up behind him, forcing him to stay in place and confront the fiery redheaded woman.

"What?" Bannack asked.

"You didn't tell Loralia that you were leaving?"

"Um."

"You just left her? You brought her to her house, she brought you inside, and then you just ran away?"

"Is that all she told you?"

It was bad enough that they knew that he had run out on Loralia. Bannack didn't want to think that she had shared with them everything that had happened leading up to him gathering his clothes and running harder and faster than he could ever remember running in his life.

"Oh, no," Eden said, shaking her head with a spiteful half-smile on her face, "but I don't think that my baby is old enough to hear that story more than once in the same evening."

"I thought that you said you didn't bond with her," Pyra accused from behind him.

"I didn't," Bannack insisted.

"Not completely," Eden said, and then mercifully stopped.

"I know what I did was awful," Bannack said, taking a step toward Eden as the other two women ran up to them, "and I want to make it up to her. I'm dealing with my own issues, but I'm working through them and I don't want to hurt her any more than I already have. I want to tell her how sorry I am before we leave."

"Well that's really sweet, Bannack, but it's not going to be quite that easy."

"Why?"

"She left," Zuri said.

Bannack felt like a rock hit his stomach.

"What do you mean she left?"

"After she told us what you did, she decided that she didn't want to be here anymore. She said there's nothing for her up here and that she wanted to go back home where she didn't have anyone to hurt her."

"Damn it."

"What are you going to do?" Ty asked as Bannack walked around the human women in the direction of the forest.

"I have to go find her."

7

I had only been away from my home for a matter of hours, but it somehow seemed like I had been gone for months. Everything seemed cold and empty, like the cavern itself had forgotten what it was like to have the touch and presence of a living creature inside of it. Even though I had lived in that cavern since birth, I entered into it with a sense of trepidation hovering just in the back of my mind. Nervousness pricked at me as I slid down through the hole in forest floor just above the mirrored realm and made my way down the large tree toward the reflected branches that made roots across the sky that had become the floor.

Something had changed within me and suddenly I didn't know where I fit anymore. The walls and crevices that had always welcomed me and had never inspired even a moment of fear now seemed strange and I wondered if I was going to be able to continue on with my solitary life in the way that I had for so many years. It was amazing how much something as simple as stepping above the ground and experiencing the presence, companionship, compassion, and betrayal of other creatures could change everything that

I knew about myself, the world, and my perceptions of existence within it.

I slid down the vines on the tree, letting them carry me until my feet hit the solid wood of the tree branches. I looked down at the reflected sky, the black expanse streaked with the murky, pinkish grey clouds that broke up the sky and muted the stars both above and below me. For the first time I found it as strange as the Klimnu, the Denynso, and the humans had found it. I had always known that our world was a mirror of the one above it, and that what we saw was not what they did, but it wasn't until I had actually stepped onto the ground and saw, for the first time in my entire existence, the sky stretch over my head rather than at my feet that I felt the odd tug within me that said I was questioning something.

Just as I had told Elianna when she nearly fell into the sky through the stone floor I had created for them by reflecting the wall behind them into the expanse in front of them, the entire existence of my kind was based on belief and trust. We had to believe from the very first moments that we drew breath that what we saw was what it was, that it would behave the way that it was meant to, and to never question it. Questioning, wondering, even for a moment, could mean death. In not questioning, however, we never encountered the possibility that what we thought we were reflecting, how we were perceiving a situation, could possibly be wrong.

I was wondering about that now as I stood at the very edge of the reflected sky and pondered what it was that I was seeing. If that was the reflection of the sky, did that mean it was only the reflection of the sky as I perceived it? What if I didn't believe that it was the sky, that I believed it was glass, would that make a difference in how it behaved?

Could it be that what I was seeing was not actually what was on the floor of the caverns, but what was being reflected by the caverns, meaning that there was something else actually there?

I knelt down by the edge of the sky and experimented by dipping my hand down into it. Like it always had, my hand slipped beneath the edge of the tree and into the cold space. I withdrew it and reached for one of the clouds. Holding tightly to the vine, I leaned slightly forward so that I could scoop my hand through the pink and grey streak that was like a faint wash of paint across the blackness. When I pulled my palm back, I watched as the pink and grey melted into cold water against my skin. It was just as I would expect it to be.

I sat back against the tree and closed my eyes. I remembered what I had thought I felt when I was standing in front of Bannack. In him I had seen the same desire and need for me that I had felt for him. I had believed that that desire was as intense and irresistible for him as the feeling that I had when I looked at him. I could only believe that because I had no other option but to believe it. Now, though, I realized that I did have another option. I could question what I believed about Bannack, and if I could question that, I could question what I believed about everything, including that the sky was all that existed on the floor of the cavern. Holding onto that feeling about Bannack, the realization that what I had seen in him wasn't really what was inside him, but what I wanted to see, I opened my eyes again and looked at the floor of the cavern.

This time I didn't see the sky. When I looked at it in those dark, silent moments I saw a pane of glass. No longer were the stars struggling to glimmer through the clouds. Instead, I saw only darkness, as if I was looking through it into the abyss deeper in the planet. I closed my eyes again, took a breath, and when I opened them I saw an expanse of thick, white ice.

I reached out over the ice and felt the cold rising up off of it, tingling against the skin of my palm. Releasing the vine that had been tethering me to the tree, I stood and stepped out onto the ice. The cold was almost painful against the bare bottoms of my feet, but I reveled in it, enjoying the sharp, undeniable feeling that told me I had created what I wanted to from my own perceptions. What I had told Elianna was absolutely true. She hadn't believed that the floor would be solid, so it turned back into what she had been told it was, and what she believed it to be, the sky. When I believed that sky to no longer be the sky, but glass, it had become glass. And now it was ice.

I didn't need my mirrored compact anymore to create what I desired. I only had to believe in my ability to change my perceptions and the perceptions of those around me, and I could create whatever I desired.

I walked across the ice until I reached the expanse of dark ground on the other side and continued forward, not glancing back over my shoulder to find out what happened to the ice when I looked away. The corners of the cavern still looked strange, but I forced myself not to look at them. I kept my eyes focused ahead and climbed my way down into the second chamber so that I could go back into my house.

The solar panels hadn't had the chance to power the lamps since I had left, so I had to rely on the soft glow from my skin to illuminate the room around me. I walked into my bedroom and removed my dress, not bothering to dress again as I made my way out of my house and toward the hot spring toward the back of the chamber that I had adopted as my bath. I sank down into the water, allowing it to soothe my muscles and ease the tension that had built within me.

I dipped my head back into the water to wash my hair and then braided it into a long plait down my back, and then twisting it up so that I could knot it around itself. The air of the cavern was cool around me as I climbed up out of the hot water and made my way back to my house, allowing my skin to dry as I walked. I felt like I was moving through a still, untouchable image, as if nothing was moving with me or responding to my presence. It was as if the emptiness inside me had extended out and taken the energy and light from everywhere I ventured.

Once I was back inside my house I reached into the bureau against my bedroom wall and pulled out a night-gown. I was just dropping it down over my head, intending to crawl into my bed and allow the world to disappear around me, when I heard a voice echoing through the cavern.

8

"**L**oralia!"

Bannack wrapped his arm through the vines hanging from the trees and called out to Loralia again. His eyes were focused on the massive expanse of ice that stretched across the cavern where the reflection of the sky had been when he was last in the underground world. He screamed for her again, not sure if he should even attempt to step on the ice, and remembering what she had said about believing in the reflection in order for it to be real. Considering he had no idea what it could possibly be reflecting in order to appear as a block of ice, he couldn't bring himself to believe in its ability to withstand his weight.

Finally Loralia appeared on the other side of the expanse much as she had the first time he saw her. Her body gave off the same soft glow, but this time it wasn't being entranced by the glow that made him want desperately to cross the cavern and be near her. This time it was knowing that she was inside that glow, emanating it from her smooth, soft skin and her hypnotic eyes that made him need to get over to her. He could feel his body responding with almost painful intensity and his heart pounded just knowing that she was close again.

"Bannack?"

Her voice sounded confused and she didn't step any closer to him.

"Loralia," he said again, "I need to talk to you."

"I don't have anything to say to you," she said.

The words made him feel like his heart had constricted and he couldn't force any breath into his lungs.

"Please," he said, taking a step down the trunk of the tree and toward the edge of the ice, "I just want to tell you that I'm sorry. If after that you want me to leave and not ever come back down here, I will. It will be the hardest thing I ever do in my life, but I'll do it if that's what you want, as long as you just let me talk to you for a few minutes now."

Loralia looked down at the ice and saw it breaking. Long, fine cracks appeared across the surface, forming patterns like lace until the pieces started to melt away, disappearing into the blackness of what was once again the reflected sky. She had created the ice to keep him away, but the sound of his voice and the desperation in his words told him that she hadn't been wrong about what she had reflected from him. It was questioning it that had brought her to the truth, however, just like questioning the sky had brought her to the ice that now melted into the stars. She wondered if outside it was raining.

"Please, Loralia," Bannack said again, "Let me come over to you."

There was a moment of stillness between them and Bannack watched as her eyes explored the sky that now stretched across the cavern, and then lift to him. He was worried that she was just going to tell him to leave and that he would never see her again, or maybe that she would make a floor for him to walk across and then make it fall away right when he was in the middle of the room so that he disappeared to wherever Jem had gone when he fell during the battle. To be honest, he really wouldn't have blamed Loralia if she decided to do either. He realized now how horribly he had treated her, and if she refused to have anything to do with him after it, it would be completely justified.

Loralia's slim, graceful hand lifted slowly to her neck and rested on her compact for a few seconds before she loosened the chain and took the small silver compact in her hand. She opened it and focused it on the wall behind him just as she had the first time that he saw her. The sky disappeared, replaced by the dark grey of the stone.

"Is it safe?" he asked.

"Is it?"

Bannack knew exactly why she was asking. She had already done what she could do to get him across to her, just as she had done everything she could to reach out to him and connect them. Now it was up to him. He had to trust in the solidity of the floor beneath his feet just as he had to trust in himself and in her. If he didn't, there would be no way for them ever to be together.

Taking a deep breath and keeping his eyes focused on Loralia's, Bannack stepped forward. The ground was solid beneath his feet and he continued ahead. He walked in silence, crossing to her with deliberate slowness to prove his absolute trust and confidence in the floor and in her. When he was within a few steps of the edge of the expanse, he stopped and reached his hands out to her. This would be the moment, the moment when he would lose his trust and fall victim to the struggle within him again, the moment when he would let the conflict inside him rise again and send him tumbling down into the sky.

Instead, the ground stayed secure. He didn't waiver in his desire to have her in his arms and as she stepped forward to join him on the solid stone that had replaced the sky. He knew that as long as she was there with him, the stone would stay exactly where it was. The sky was transient, always changing and shifting, never staying the same as if it didn't know exactly what it wanted to be. The stone, though, was absolute and definite. It was strong and solid, and never changed.

This is what he felt now as Loralia walked toward him, reaching out to rest her cool, soft fingers against his palms so that he could hold them and draw her forward into his arms. What had once been transient like the sky was now like the stone, and he would never again allow himself to deny her, even for a moment.

"I'm sorry," he whispered into her hair as he cradled her against his chest.

Loralia pressed herself closer against him and he heard a gentle sigh slip from her lips.

"You don't have to wonder who you are, Bannack," she said.

The words struck him and he leaned back to look at her.

"What do you mean?"

"You worry that you don't fit what you are supposed to be; that you don't live up to what people expect of you. You wonder if you are really who everyone has always told you that you are, or that you should be."

It was something that Bannack had never expressed to anyone, a feeling that he had carried within him his entire life and never given voice to, even to his closest family and friends. He understood now that it was not her that had caused all of his struggle, but himself. It wasn't that he was upset about her being another species that he didn't know anything about, but that he didn't know himself well enough to trust that he could be the mate that she deserved.

"You are a warrior, just as you were born to be. You are strong, you are brave, and you are powerful."

As she spoke, Loralia's hands drifted from Bannack's shoulders down his chest. He felt her fingers exploring his body through the fabric of his clothing as if memorizing the curves and planes so that she could remember them even when they were apart. He wrapped his arms around her waist, pulling her against him so that she could feel more of his body and how much he needed her. Suddenly she drew in a breath and looked down.

"What is it?" he asked softly.

"Did I do something wrong? Did I try to go too fast?"

Her voice sounded thin, almost like she was afraid to ask him the questions. He took her hands in his, pulling them off of his chest and holding them between them, giving them a slight shake so that she would look at him. He hated that she thought that it was her fault that he had run away from her, and he was going to do everything that he could to show her that it wasn't true.

9

———

The look in Bannack's eyes nearly took my breath away as he stared deeply at me. His eyes were flickering from their usual greyish blue shade to orange and back, and I could feel intense, searing heat pulsating from his body. It was so hot I felt like it should have burned me. Instead, it tingled across my skin and made my breath deepen.

"You did nothing wrong," Bannack said.

His voice was low and rumbling, deeper than it had been any other time he had spoken to me.

"Are you sure?"

Bannack glanced down at my lips and then back into my eyes. Without saying anything, he leaned forward and caught my mouth with his. The kiss was even deeper, more intense than our first, like it was going beyond his lips against mine to connect us on another level. As his mouth moved against mine, he pulled me closer and I could feel the hardness of his body pressing against my belly. My breath caught in my throat and I arched my back to push more firmly against it. Bannack let out a soft groan and I started guiding him off of the stone and toward the second chamber of the cavern. I wanted to bring him home with me.

We walked along in silence and I could feel his passion growing with each step. I led him past the house that I occasionally visited, where I had changed my clothes after bathing, and through the rest of the chamber toward the large, protective chamber in the back of the cavern. This was truly my home, the place where I truly felt the most comfortable and the most at ease, and this was where I wanted to be with him.

"Is this your home?" he asked as we stepped into the chamber.

"Yes," I told him, "I have a house, but this is where I consider myself at home. This is where I feel safe."

Bannack gave my wrist a gentle tug so that I curled back into his arms. He pressed a kiss to the top of my head and then another to my cheekbone.

"I will keep you safe," he whispered, "I will always keep you safe."

His lips touched the side of my neck and I felt a shiver travel through my body and settle between my thighs. I ached for his touch again and could feel the warmth building as my body prepared for him. The tip of his tongue grazed across my skin. The feeling made my body tremble and I grabbed onto his upper arms, holding them to give myself stability as his mouth continued to explore along the side of my neck and down into the curve between my neck and shoulder.

I felt Bannack's hands smooth down the sides of my hips and onto my outer thighs, gathering the sides of my nightgown with his fingers so that he could slip his hands beneath the hem. He moaned as he realized that I wasn't wearing anything under the nightgown and I felt him fill his hands with my flesh, kneading gently as he met my mouth again with another intense kiss.

His mouth moved across mine with depth and need, but not intensity. He moved slowly, carefully tasting me as his hands massaged into my muscles and pulled me ever closer so that our hips met and the irresistible pressure of his erection against my belly made me whimper into his mouth. His hands swept up, tossing my nightgown aside. I had been wearing nothing else, and again I was completely bare in front of him. I reached up behind my neck and loosened the chain that held the compact I had reattached to its hook. Gently placing the compact down on top of my nightgown, I turned back to him.

"You are the most beautiful thing I have ever seen," he whispered.

"Let me see you," I whispered back, reaching forward to release the laces that tied up the front of his pants.

Bannack stepped back and took off his shirt, letting it fall to the floor beside my nightgown. He looked at me and I stepped closer to him, bringing my hands back to the laces on his pants. They loosened easily beneath my fingers and I eased his pants down his hips so that they fell to the floor. Bannack stepped out of them and took off his boots. Finally he was as bare as I was. There was nothing between us anymore and I indulged myself by touching the front of my body to his. The heat of his skin drew me in and I ran my hand down his chest and along the chiseled, rippling muscles along his side.

"You are beautiful," I said quietly, admiring every bit of him that my fingers touched.

"I know that I don't deserve to be with you," he said,

nuzzling his face in my hair, "but if you will let me, I will do everything I can to earn you. Starting with worshiping every inch of you."

With that, he swept me into his arms so that my hips nestled against his, my core cradling his erection and my breasts crushed against his chest. I wrapped my arms around his neck and my legs around his waist. He was so tall that holding me like that had me several feet off of the ground, but I wasn't afraid. I knew that I was never safer than when I was in his arms.

"How did your kind choose a life mate?" he asked, his labored breath making his voice low and sultry.

He held me with such ease, seeming to need to put forth no effort to keep me nestled against him. His mouth dropped to the side of my neck again and I closed my eyes briefly to savor the feeling.

"They were tied together," I finally managed to say.

"Tied?" he asked, lifting his mouth just long enough to speak before kissing along my collarbone.

I nodded, tilting my head back to encourage his mouth to my neck again.

"The women wove braids out of pieces of cloth and a treasured friend would tie their wrists together and say a blessing over them."

"Will you do that with me?" he asked, his lips tracing along the front of my neck until they reached the soft dip between my collarbones.

"Yes," I said, leaning back a little further to grant him more access.

"Until then, can I show you how the Denynso bond?"
"Yes."

Bannack tightened his grip on me and started to walk

forward. By the direction he was moving I knew he was headed toward the long, low bench that ran along the far wall. A few moments later he lowered himself to his knees and rested me back against the plush cushions, carefully drawing my legs from around his waist so that he could sit back on his feet. He gently parted my thighs, draping one leg over the side of the bench and the other over his shoulder so that I was totally open and vulnerable to him.

"This time," he said, running his hand down my thigh toward the wet heat he had been creating with every touch and every kiss, "when I touch you, I want to be looking at you."

Just those words made me feel like I was edging beyond my control and I pushed my hips closer to him, opening further to surrender myself completely to him. Bannack brought his hand the rest of the way down and drew the pads of his fingers through my core, sending shivers through my body. He pressed deeper, parting my folds so he could explore me as he gazed into my face.

I watched as Bannack dipped his fingers into his mouth, drawing them across his tongue before reaching down again and slipping them into me. I gasped at the feeling, so overwhelmed that I at once tried to pull away from it and push deeper into it. He moved patiently, easing his fingers deeper into my tight, untouched body and moving them slowly so that he massaged my upper wall. He groaned in response to my body arching up toward him and the whimpers pouring from my chest. I gripped his arm, digging my fingers deeply into him as he continued his deliciously torturous exploration.

Almost unbearable pressure was building throughout my belly, thighs, and hips and I felt the same desperate need for him that I had in the house in the Denynso compound before he left. Just before he allowed the tension to release, however, he carefully withdrew his fingers. I gasped at the emptiness and searched his face, worried for a moment that he was going to leave again. He smiled at me and drew his fingers through his mouth again, removing my slick fluids from his skin.

"Not yet," he whispered, "Be patient."

I wasn't feeling particularly patient, but I nodded, willing to give all of my trust and control over to him and allow him to guide me. I wanted to please him in whatever way he wanted, and whatever way that I could. He eased my leg down off of his shoulder at the same time that he took my hand and gently led me up into a sitting position. I moved by instinct when he stood, lowering myself to my knees in front of him. Bannack stroked my face tenderly before tucking his hand around behind my head and guiding me forward so that I opened my mouth and welcomed his erection in against my tongue.

His long, hard shaft felt incredible in my mouth, and the deep sounds rolling over me like thunder pushed me even further. I let my mouth glide along him, savoring the feeling of every ridge and vein, and the warm, salty taste of his skin. I felt like I could have continued on like that for the rest of the night, but suddenly Bannack's hand tightened on my head and he gently pulled me back away from him. I looked up at him and he eased me to my feet.

Bannack sat on the bench behind him and drew me forward until I straddled his hips much as I had in the house, but this time I was facing him rather than looking away. Wrapping one arm around my hips, he lowered me down toward his lap. I felt the tip of his erection touch my opening and drew in a breath. He paused only for a moment, then led me the rest of the way down so that I settled against him, enveloping his shaft deep within me. My head dropped back and my mouth opened to cry out, but there was no sound. The feeling of him filling me so completely was so intense I could only gasp for breath.

We sat still for several seconds as my body adjusted to holding him.

"Relax for me," he whispered.

I lifted my head so that I could look into his eyes again. Letting his beautiful face soothe me, I relaxed my muscles and let him sink even deeper into me. His hands came to my hips and he began to guide them, rolling them in slow circles. Bannack sat up straighter so that our bodies touched and rested his hand on my lower back. Bracing himself against the bench with his other hand, he rocked my hips into a faster rhythm. As our bodies moved and slipped across each other our sounds blended and swirled, filling the space around us until I could perceive nothing but what we were creating together.

His body nurtured me back into the sense of dizzying pressure, but this time the desperation wasn't there. I had him within me and I couldn't imagine there was anything more incredible. Suddenly, though, I realized Bannack began to grunt deeply and thrust intensely up into me, coaxing me closer to the edge of my control, and then pushing me over so that I screamed his name and contracted around him at the same moment that he cried out, throbbing and pulsing as hot streams filled me.

I held Bannack as tightly as I could, letting my tremors embrace him as he continued to pulse within my body. I sobbed for breath and clung to him, burying my fingers in his hair and rocking my hips subtly as I rode out the last waves of my climax. His mouth slowly trailed down onto my breast and suckled at one nipple, then the other, before lifting up to cover mine.

We kissed languidly as our bodies cooled and then he parted our lips to nuzzle his nose against mine.

"Come home with me."

10

———

Bannack kept his eyes closed as he asked the question, part of him worried that Loralia wouldn't be as willing to go back above ground, and that he might have to try to get used to living down in her world. When she didn't answer, he opened his eyes to look at her. He saw her eyes widen and he smiled.

"They change color after we've found our mate," he explained, knowing that the orange of his eyes had surprised her.

As much as it had worried him that he was going to have to learn about an entirely new species in order to be with her, he realized that it felt completely natural to explain the Denynso to her and let her explain her kind to him. He enjoyed discovering the new things about her and looked forward to each new detail that he would uncover in their lives together. She still hadn't answered his question and he looked directly into her eyes, trying to make the connection that the Denynso were able to make with their mates. He didn't hear anything.

Tilting his head quizzically at her, he tried harder to make the connection.

"What?" she asked.

"What are you thinking right now?"

"What do you mean?"

"What are you thinking right now?" he repeated.

"That that was incredible," she admitted, "and wondering how long it will be until we can do it again."

He laughed softly.

"Soon," he told her.

"Why did you want to know what I was thinking?"

"When my kind find our mates and bond, our minds connect. We're able to reach each other's thoughts and communicate just by thinking. I can't hear your thoughts."

"So I'm not your mate?"

Loralia sounded devastated and confused, and Bannack felt her start to pull away from him. He held her tighter and pulled her against him again.

"No, no. You are. If you weren't, my eyes wouldn't have changed. We just can't read each other's thoughts."

"Could it be because I'm not a Denynso?"

"The human women are able to communicate with their mates."

Bannack worried that she was going to be upset, but she smiled at him.

"I guess you are just going to have to settle for trusting and loving me."

"I do," he replied.

"Which one?"

The smile had faded from her lips and she was looking at him in a way that felt like she was looking into his soul.

"Both. I trust you," he leaned forward and touched a kiss to the middle of her chest, "and I love you."

"I love you, too."

Their mouths met again and he drew her as close to his body as he could. He was still buried deep within her and he felt himself hardening again. Loralia began to roll her hips slowly, and he carefully turned her, resting her on her back and coming down on top of her.

TWO DAYS later Bannack stood in the row of warriors in the meeting hall, his eyes fixed on Creia even though his thoughts were focused on the table behind him. He knew Loralia was sitting there among the human women, gazing at his back. Even though he still couldn't listen to her thoughts or communicate with her with his mind, he could feel her. He could sense her presence and it was at once empowering and soothing. With her near him he was calm and in control, but felt stronger and more powerful than he ever had.

"Many times we have come to this room to honor the courage and bravery of our warriors," Creia said from his platform, "but tonight it is for a different reason. Our men have walked into battle without fear and have come back victorious. They have always protected our home and our kind, and have offered up their lives to ensure we can live comfortably. Tonight they prepare for a challenge that none have faced. Tomorrow these warriors will leave the compound and be the first Denynso to venture out onto Uoria. We don't know what adversities they may encounter or what threats they will find. Tonight we feast for tomorrow we watch them walk toward something even more frightening than the risk of death: the unknown. I know that each of them is prepared and that they will show the same strength, determination, and mastery that they have in everything else that they have done."

Bannack's spine straightened even further at his king's words. He dreaded leaving Loralia after having just found her, but now more than ever he understood the need for their journey. He had promised her that he would keep her safe, and he intended to do everything in his power to ensure that he kept that promise.

TBC

(To be continued in Part III...)